Grizzly Itch: An unBEARable itch which
you cannot reach

BEWARE OF
BEARS!

For Mum, Dad, Alice,
Nana and Pop Pops, with love.

First published 2019 by Macmillan Children's Books
an imprint of Pan Macmillan
The Smithson, 6 Briset Street, London, EC1M 5NR
Associated companies throughout the world
www.panmacmillan.com

ISBN 978-1-5290-1356-6 (HB)
ISBN 978-1-5290-1357-3 (PB)

1 3 5 7 9 8 6 4 2

A CIP catalogue record for this book
is available from the British Library.

Printed in China

THE GRIZZLY ITCH

Victoria Cassanell

MACMILLAN CHILDREN'S BOOKS

Something woke Bear up from his long winter sleep . . .

He had an itch.
It was unBEARable.

He just

couldn't

reach it –

it was a GRIZZLY itch.

Luckily, Bear knew a tree that was perfect for scratching.
The only problem was . . .

. . . it was VERY busy.

Bear waited . . .

and waited . . .

and then waited some more . . .

Until it was finally his turn.

But then . . .

suddenly . . .

CR

ASH!

"What have you done?" cried Bear.
"That was the only tree that could scratch my itch!

And this is no ordinary itch –
It's a GRIZZLY itch!"

"I'm sorry Bear," said Beaver.
"I was going to use it for my dam.
But don't worry, I know *lots* of good
trees, I'll help you find another one."

Bear didn't like the first tree.
"It's not very friendly!"

"Never mind," said Beaver.
"Plenty more trees in the forest!"

But the next tree made
Bear feel a bit shy . . .

The next tree
wasn't a tree.

And the next tree buzzed.

“Now this is a lovely tree,
right next to the river,” said Beaver.
“And it looks nice and quiet up there.”

So Bear climbed up.
"It *is* nice and quiet up here."

But Bear wobbled a bit,
then wobbled a lot.

And then . . .

SPLASH!

"It's no good," said Bear, sadly, "we'll never find a new tree. Now I've got a grizzly itch *and* I'm wet!"

"There, there," said Beaver.

"OH!"

"up a bit!"

"down a bit!"

"sideways a bit!"

"Better?" said Beaver. "*Much* better," replied Bear.
"My grizzly itch has gone!"

Bear was so happy, he decided to do something kind for Beaver. He picked up his old scratching tree: "Let's use it for your dam!"

"Thank you for your help," said Beaver,
"and for letting me borrow your tree."
"You're welcome," said Bear.
"Now it's *our* tree."

BEWARE OF
BEARS!

Grizzly Itch: An itch that only a friend can scratch